DEDICATED TO COURTNEY FROM CHAYLA MAYLA

Copyright @ 2020 by Chayla Cooper of Sleeq Productions
Illustrations by Waqas Ahmed
Manufactured in the United States of America. All rights reserved
For information address Sleeq Productions at:
www.SleeqProductions.com or SleeqProductions@Gmail.com

First Edition, First Print 2020

ISBN-13: 978-0-9966605-2-5

Summary: Romans 12:5-6 states, "So in Christ we, though many, form one body, and each member belongs to all the others. We have different gifts, according to the grace given to each of us…"

In a world full of comparison, it is important to impart to children at a young age that no matter your differences in this world, you are important and play a role in the body of Christ. Your gifts may be different from those around you, but that does not make you lesser than anyone.

A follow up to Chayla Cooper's book "Thank You God", "You Belong" continues to utilize Christian teachings by following a young ant who is about to embark on a journey into the unknown and doesn't understand why God would choose her when her gifts aren't as great as those around her. With the help of her mother, she realizes that she too has great attributes that are needed in the kingdom and to trust God along her journey.

No part of this publication may be reproduced, distributed, or transmitted in any form or by any means, including photocopying, recording, or other electronic or mechanical methods, without the prior written permission of the publisher, except in the case of brief quotations embodied in critical reviews and certain other noncommercial uses permitted by copyright law. For permission, request contact author at website above.

Ordering Information:
Quantity sales. Special discounts are available on quantity purchases by corporations, associations, and others. For details, contact publisher at the email/website above.

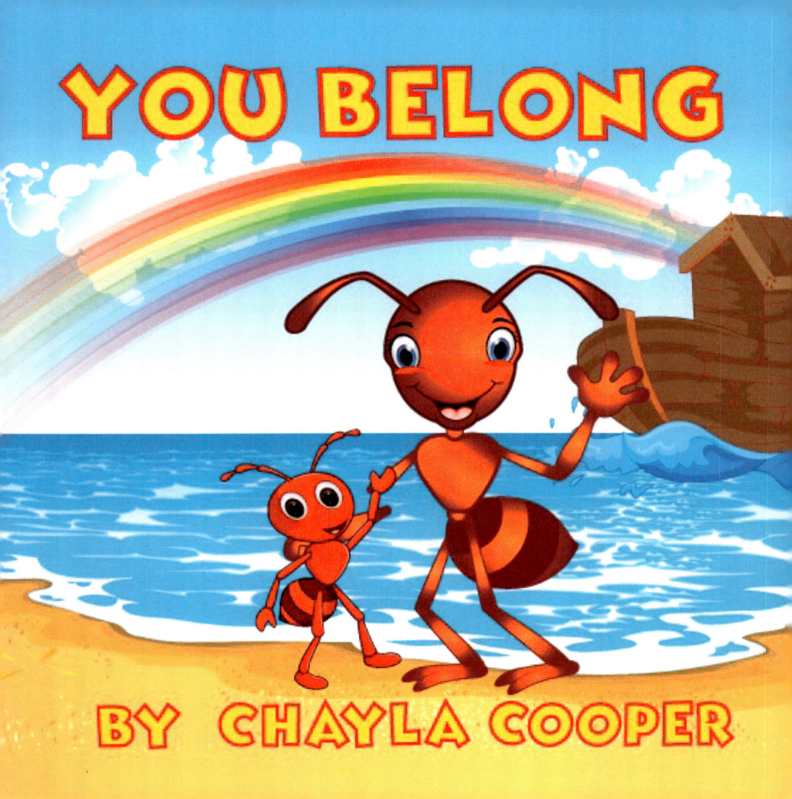

Did you hear? God told Noah to build an ark!
He's sending big rain and soon it will start.

He invited every animal to come two by two,
From the birds of the air, the lions that roam,
The monkeys in the trees, and little ants like you!

But why would God want me? I'm just a little ant!
Fly gracefully in the air, I surely can't.

Swing from a tree, that's not me.
Roar mighty and loud, I can't make a sound.
It's just little me, I'm one in the crowd.

You're super strong I must say.
And the way you move so fast, we get out the way.

The way that you think, you're super smart.
And you care for your family with all of your heart.

You're special and loved in every way. You belong on the ark, no matter what you say! So go live an adventure, go be great. Hurry up now, you have no time to wait! And don't forget to listen to what God has to say, And remember He made you perfect in every way.

THE END

Made in the USA
Columbia, SC
15 September 2020